Poetry My Mother Would Not Have Approved

(And other writings)

Poetry My Mother Would Not Have Approved

1919-2008

<WARNING: You must be 35 years or older to continue>

Contents

Other Writings

Contents

Introduction

In Poetry My Mother Would've Approved the author wrote freely of his life and perceptions. In PMMWNHA he continues the same way adding more of the sublime ideal to the earthly poetry of its predecessor. His attitude in his poetry is "take the impulse to create put it to paper, napkin, parchment, fresco, business card, backside of a magazine etc. then finish the thought as gracefully and truthfully as it deserves.

Poetry composed of magnificent words and erudite phrases can be impressive, even compelling, but unless these artifices contribute to the perception of a bonafide sentiment there is no place for them, and in his poetic words all of the unnecessary, pedantic and diffuse are struck from Van Heyden's literature.

Editor
Frank A. Carlyle

Preface

I chose to dedicate this volume of poetry to G. Casanova since a small percent of living persons can claim they are familiar with his intellectual gifts and philanthropic tendencies rather than his "reputation".

At first that may seem a contradiction since this volume surely contains in the main poems and writings about the sentiments and peculiarities of the subject we call "sex". For many the subject is one of cross currents, uncertainties and subconscious associations with birth, STDs, dire failures to attract attention, and general inhibitions about communicating it and its appurtenances. It is for that exact reason that poetry, in its lofty composition, and its altitude in the literary world, is the perfect conveyance to exalt the subject and put it in a proper perspective, as Casanova's contributions to the culture of Man have not been so arranged.

This book of poetry is dedicated to
Giacomo Casanova

Poetry My Mother Would Not Have Approved

(And other writings)

Maiden's Ode To Sex

May my lover's testes swell
With glorious sperm for me
And his artful rod
Be stiff as steel in wintry.

May his semen flow unabated
to my soothing canal,
While I caress his sweated chest
With golden strands.

And laugh out loud the rush
And kiss his fumbling hands.

Blueberry Muffin,

Sometimes I want a blueberry muffin,
Large that comes straight from the oven.
That kind, and sweet but not too sweet,
With lots of butter too.

Sometimes I want a woman, a
Healthy woman, supple and thin,
One that can be sexy,
Strong though feminine within.

Sometimes I want to go fast,
Very very fast.
The kind of fast would shock
Most and even dismay.

There is no substitute
For the blueberry muffin,
The healthy woman, or
For going fast, I pray.

Ferris Bueler's Wedding

...And do you Katherine, accept his sometimes corny jokes as well as his chivalrous deeds and sincere efforts to make you comfortable?

Yes...

And do you accept Ferris' hardness as well as his love, which often come simultaneously?
Yes.

And Ferris do you take Katherine's sometimes ditsy flights of fancy in the same spirit you take her meaningful looks and passionate embraces?

<Quizzical smile> Yes!

And Ferris do you accept responsibility when Katherine serves up cold slop for dinner with same resolve and fair sense of play as when she spends all day making a fabulous four course meal?

<Laughs> Pretty sure I can do that.

Good, and Katherine are you willing to slave over a hot stove or risk exploding some eggs in a microwave to make sure that Ferris is well fed no matter what?

<Laughing> I do. Etc, etc.

Somnambulance

Dear Queen give

The knight his night.

He deserves it well,

His valor pure.

And then do not dally,

Do not temporize,

For you are the King's

For life, his prize.

If I had no hands

If I had no hands
I could not hold your face
Lovingly; I could not trace
The charming contour; I would
Not feel the generous warmth;
You could not receive my ineffable
Admiration; nor would you
Have the soft memory of my touch.

Not Necessarily A Dream

And somewhere a man is

Holding your beautiful face,

His hands so gently padding

Its cheeks with

Soft... and —

There, and there and

Everywhere with

Soft Kisses and

Putting his lips to

Your lips one

Molecule at a time

And it takes forever

These moments to

Arrive — it takes forever

And I wait and we wait,

But it takes forever

These moments to arrive.

Poem written by a young boy to an even younger girl in Florence Italy circa 1523

Why won't you marry me?
You look like you could
Use a good lay.
You're always flirting with me.

Your moon sized eyes
Dispel any thought you're
A cold virgin, and what's
More your hands are hot.

Hey, 'you like cunnilingus?
Well that's my specialty!
You say you love big
Flamboyant hard-ons?
Well I've got one!

Even your Mother likes me.
And now that I've
Got my own horse,
We can go riding
And sliding together.

So why don't you marry me. . .
O great, you will!
That a girl.
Ahhhhhhh!I knew you wanted to.

When

When shall we find
Ourselves in each other's
Arms delivering long
Beautiful kisses to our
Bodies, and when are you
Going to wrap those
Fine legs around me?

I'll hungrily wait to
Penetrate your womanly
Secrets, when our tongues
Will engage passionate war
While trembling hands
Reach for Ecstasy
Never approached before.

To have the tips of your
Smoldering breasts
Press burning to my chest.
Your womanhood covets
My potency,
Descending the warm pink
Innocence, enclosing enveloping
Slowly disappearing into
Quickened heartbeats and
Breathless sighs.

For though I
Know you not well
I feel I could know you
Better than any other ever has.

The sex I like. . .

The sex I like is
The kind after which
There I am lying
In the wistful
Philosophic thoughts
About the nature
Of God and existence. . .

Bellowous Boy

I spread the cheeks of

flaming fannies, I

Ungirth garters of

Glorious gals.

I'm a Bellowous boy of

Mellifluous moods,

I am your Bounty

Filled with Joy.

Strategy

Recently I put my emotions in a jar

And left the lid slightly open.

So those who want to see and know

More about me can do so with ease,

While I can prevent any complete

Disclosure with only a superficial

Movement of my hand.

SUPERBOWLS

Openings
In the line are
Not just "openings"
They're super holes.

AND lest we forget
Everything at
The SUPERBOWL
Is likewise
Superior:

Cheerleaders are
Super-girls
The players are
Super-men,

(Hot) Dogs are
Super-hot
And beverages
Super-cold.

Cheers are
Super-CHEERS
And beers
SUPER beers.

If played in
Florida
The mascots are
Komodo Dragons,

Which we know are
SUPER-LIZARDS.

Touchdowns known
As a T-D
Are reported
As S-TDs!

And so it goes
For Everything is SUPER
At SUPERBOWLS.

How long is a second?

The time it takes to flip a light switch.

The time it takes to snap fingers twice.

Drop a penny on a table from ten inches.

Say "Thank You".

Say "Goodbye".

Say "I had a nice time".

One half to one third the time most TV's turn on,

And the time it takes to turn it off.

The time it takes to knock on a closed door before entering.

The time it takes to smile at a stranger who is looking at you.

What Chance the Fall Leaf

Pulled down to earth by gravity,
Soaked and weighed down by rains.
Blown down by gusts mightily.
What chance for a leaf remains?

Like a leaf are we?

When chill wind of misfortune
Blows mysterious
Upon our saddened face,
When torrents of error
Condemn us to disgrace.
And obligation's weight
Bears semblance to
A Mountain of slate,
What chance have we?

Out of the dark and
Nebulous dreams that
Come to haunt us,
From twists of fate
Calamities insult us,

When regret itself
Is no longer salve
For life's injuries
That pierce us,

What then are we?
The Fall leaf?
Who are we—
Who are we indeed!

What are we,
Regarded so anonymously—
Handled so ignominiously.
That we should be treated
So indifferently?

None but the wisest,
The strongest, the best,
Suited to oppose the
Arrows & Strings of
Outrageousness.

None but the most
Cunning and none but
The most deserving.

The leaf, like any other
Life has its chances.
We have our chances.
Do we not?

Wind Chimes

Can you hear that-

Can you hear that tinkling?

The tintinnabulating treasure of Sound.

Wind chimes.

When I think about them I feel good.

The wind blows,

The chimes *speak* to me.

I'm quieted.

Back down the centuries to a Village,

In Asia I'm reminded of another time, and

Another place,

When the wind blew

Across a mountain top overlooking a verdant

Valley bustling with happy people.

Erectile Stipulation

And she winked,

"Why don't we to bed"?

"My penis", I said,

"Is reserved for Venus,

And you are nar' but a

Reflecting moon of her."

Girls Who Giggle

I love girls who giggle and
I like girls who can wiggle.
But I don't care for girls who
Can *only* wiggle and giggle.

I'M HOT, I'M HOT

I'm very VERY hot.

I know you're not,
 I know you're really not.

To get this note from me,
But do not take it as a tease.

I only mean to please.
When I move between your knees,
I'm really not a sleaze.

I'm hot I'm HOT
For such a honey pot.

I Do I DON'T Understand

I'm shaving today and I notice the setting for the shaving blades hasn't changed in 37 years... well not exactly, since the manufacturer didn't make an electric razor with adjustable blade depth 37 years ago.

One day long time ago I tried adjusting those blades to see which setting was the best. There's nine of them. That's right <u>nine</u> different separate settings.

The only one that worked for me was #9, the deepest setting -the one with the most blade showing, similar thing to a table saw except that facial hair is pretty easy to cut once it gets above the surface of the skin.

So, I'm thinking what are those other eight settings doing there — who's running around with a (1) or (2) setting, must be pretty effeminate because my whiskers aren't all that stiff compared to some guys I know!

It's not the same with a lawn mower 'cause there you want some of the grass left above the ground and the settings give you a choice how much, you see?

And that concept definitely wouldn't work for the ladies. Women want it all gone. In fact, gals would be so much happier if it didn't grow at all.

There's nothing more useless to a woman than hair on her knee caps, unless it's a man who uses a ⌘ 1 setting on his shaver.

Other writings

Technocratic Future

Someday we'll even see a showerhead that moves with the showeree, using infrared technology with a manual shut-off of course. Just imagine a shower that automatically adjusts the temperature of and the direction of flow of the water! Then later there'll be voice activated styles of and intensity of pressure settings. But fortunately you'll still have to do the washing and scrubbing (or someone you well know). There'll be a "bouquet" setting, a 'Niagara' setting, a pulsing of course and the always popular needle stimulator for the quick morning wake ups. And of course an auto shut-off when you depart the shower compartment.

Our technocratic world enlarges every day. With new gadgets to do and with which to communicate better, and that is a good thing. In the not too distant future some of us will use hover cars to get to and from assignments. Where ground transportation would take several hours between jobs or home and deployment like those for a building contractor the hover car much like helicopters employed by ranchers of large spreads will provide able service to many destinations in a fraction of the time, and reduce simultaneously the stigma of gridlock by that many fewer vehicles on the highways.

Alternate Goodbyes

When leaving a gathering for the night, instead of saying, "Have a nice evening and thanks for inviting me to the party," why not try this: "May your husband's manhood grow much stronger every day." If it is a male hosting the affair convert to: "May your wife's bosom grow fuller and more beautiful each day" And just for fun and to add a "European touch" say it pleasantly in Spanish:"De mayo los senos de su esposa crecer más completa y más bella cada día."

Sounds much nicer?

Sometimes,

I get tears easily (for practically no reason at all; and then again) for the heart-break stories, such as this famous one:

An editor once challenged authors to write a six word story. Ernest Hemingway did and this is what he wrote: *Baby shoes, for sale, never used.*

Do you get tears when you hear or read a story about the overcoming of human suffering? Or the overcoming of inadequate education? Those are the kind of tears I like to shed.

And even the simple act of seeing someone get what they have long dreamed for?

Have you ever experienced the joy of relief and new found energy when after a bout with flue or a long convalescence has ended?

What of a time when you mastered a skill that even you were on tenterhooks about?

I'm sure that you'll agree, if you can recollect any of these, that they are truly among the great reasons life is worth living.

No Headlights

Ever try driving a car at night with the headlamps turned off? Like walking down the sidewalk blindfolded only a lot scarier.

Well, it can be done. . . by the light of a full moon as once occurred to me one night coming down from a 11,000 foot altitude road out of Denver. I decided I would drive all night through the night non-stop until I reached LA and then complete the journey the next morning. What began as an experiment turned into one of the most pleasurable and memorable experiences of my life.

Everyone loves driving cars, right? Well, yes of course provided we understand that there are no absolutes. The odd, shocking and most beautiful aspect of all is the fact that without the car headlamps on, the road ahead in full moonlight is visible for miles all illuminated to the same degree. You see, the back glare of the headlamps obscures the road further out than the beam, so turning off the headlamps suddenly and completely immerses one in a surreal world but having no hidden dangers whatsoever!

Warm was the night and warm seemed the moonlight. The two-seater Suzuki hummed along with no passenger yap yap to intrude upon the immensely satisfying quiet, enhanced by the softness of wind flowing outside and around the car. If ever there were a moment of "oneness" with nature this was that moment.

Try it sometime.

Annie Oakley Rides Again

Last year I was contemplating some rather startling discoveries about myself. Usually this doesn't happen but once or twice in a lifetime for most of us. But this was so startling and so unique that I mention it here to edify those of you who read this.

For as long as I can remember, I thought that other people were in the know about most things, for example: how to make a great catered dinner, how to make a stereo from scratch, how to paint, how to compose music and songs, how to write good fiction, even how to build a house.

Then last year, not long ago really, it came to me in a flash, literally a flash. I can do most of these things better than the people I thought knew how to do them.

Not a brag essentially, since I acknowledged it to myself alone. "Anything you can do I can do better" is a bit of a boast, but if one CAN do it better what's the sense of saying, "well. . . er. . . I guess I can do it better than you"

Are conclusions important?

Yes, otherwise this world would not exist.

Some people reach conclusions rather swiftly while others take a l-o-n-g time.

Two men are standing under a passing jet not looking above. The first man by the jet engine sound alone has already concluded that

it is a jet airplane
it is a military jet
probably a fighter
not from a nearby floating aircraft carrier
and about 2000 feet above,
its general compass direction that it is headed.

The other man has yet to decide if it is in fact a jet plane.

No conscious action, no effort is put forth by humans before a calculation and a conclusion of the effort involved. That's how important conclusions are.

Lie Down For Awhile

I'm going to lie down for awhile then
I'm going to smile for awhile, then
I'm going to rise for awhile and
Surprise for a while, even
Devise for awhile plus
Surmise for awhile.
Then I'm gonna trundle a bit
Bundle a bit and fondle a bit;
Masticate awhile,
Assimilate awhile, then I'm going to
Pollinate* for awhile and after
Contemplate for awhile.
Then I'll cleanse and purify for awhile,
Nourish the body for awhile,
Exercise for awhile and
Lie down for awhile.
Following this activity, I'm
Going to reflect for awhile,
Remit for awhile and
Restore things for awhile. Then
I'm going to smile some more,
Contemplate some more, and
Renew my goals some more,
Take what I devised for awhile and
Make it known to many for awhile.
See that all is well for awhile, and

Tell people that all is well for awhile.
Finally, I am going to consummate
My day for awhile planning the
Next day for awhile, and then
Lie down for awhile.

*But never Pontificate for awhile.

Compulsory Education-A Failure

It has been observed that anything which is done automatically is better done by hand. So it is and has been and with worsening results with education when done compulsorily. The guilds of the 12th through the 18th century were exceedingly successful in educating its apprentice students in skills necessary to carry on survival in a maturing society, raising its head from the Dark Ages.

Where we went wrong was, not in providing school houses for our children in which they could read books and ask questions of a preceptor but, in passing laws making it compulsory to attend. In fact our civilization began, almost imperceptibly, to decline the moment we as adults agreed to *be forced to* sending our children "to school" legally, and of course accepting fiscal funding through taxation for this encroachment on the rights of children and parents.

"Life is the best educator", is a saying that over and over again has been accepted by the multitudes, and this is not true in any sense. Life does not induce anyone to think better, act better, respond faster, create more: only the individual's will to conquer his environment, only the individual's determination to achieve completely that which the individual most wants to achieve is the chief inducement to think better, act better, respond faster, create more. What life does teach is what happens if one does not "get along with others." And this lesson has the apparency of being wise, when in fact it has the opposite effect. Examine the lives of any man or woman who has established themselves equitably in life, who are productive members of society, typical men and women as well as great men and women who are self-reliant, self-generated persons, and in that examination will be still found 1) the willingness to learn from their own observation and 2) competence derived from applying their willingness to observe.

When any honest research is done, the only time compulsory education worked, worked when it was used solely for military or religious purposes. Today and for the future these uses are superfluous necessities as a compulsory practice. If a person can't be trusted to align him or herself with an abiding philosophy about life then that person isn't long for this world and is a detriment to the society.

For the most part compulsory education is regimentation as it was in its inception. Men need to think freely, act freely and perceive that they are free to do so even in a society which has given in to compulsory practices such as compulsory education. We did away with conscription, finally, and likewise we would be well advised to do away with compulsory education, even compulsory health care.

What to do in their absence? That requires diligent research and testing. Which requires, naturally the self-determined, non-compulsory desire to discover and learn. Whose willing?

Is it Natural

Is it natural for a person to want to communicate aesthetically?

The answer would be in two parts:

1) Is it natural for a person to communicate?

To that I would give an emphatic <u>YES.</u>

2) What does it mean to communicate aesthetically?

Well what does aesthetics mean is next: In an aesthetic manner, Therefore we have

Aesthetic – Def. A The beautiful qualities of something (for now we'll leave out the academic definitions of "principles on which an artist's work is based".)

And what may we ask is beautiful? Great and necessary question.

Well, for a saltwater fisherman, the prospects of living in the middle of a desert would not be beautiful since it not only deprives him of his livelihood (and passion) but it also deprives him of making use of a boat and wind and seafaring conditions as a game he likes playing.

So, it is not enough to rely just on the old adage, "Beauty is in the eye of the beholder" since some people are blind and some don't perceive the world only through sight.

Beauty to be "beauty" must compliment the perceiver of it in some way. It certainly must bring added pleasure without which life is not as pleasurable or interesting.

A rodeo guy would probably shirk listening to such a sonnet. He would not find any beauty in it.

When we go out on a "date" or to an "affair" we most often want to dress properly, give a good appearance to others, and again be perceived as not being at odds with the environment. Dressing for public viewing, our appearance is after all a communication.

Then we have those who use various avenues of expression, such as music and movies and book writing to further their message or emotions about particular subjects in a way that we might very well find objectionable. However, if there are like minded persons receiving the communication via these media then the maxim yet holds true. Violently worded rap music, for example, appeals to a segment of our society. And it uses song and musical composition with its rhythm and dynamics just as a symphony by Bela Bartok or Tchaikovsky would. No doubt the originators want to communicate along the lines that are going to be pleasing to buyers of their music. And to some degree they succeed.

So, in this short essay, I have proposed a question, which may not have *ever* been proposed publicly, and answered it.

Aesthetics Is cWhere Man Ultimately Finds His Salvation

It may turn out eventually that aesthetics is where Man ultimately finds his salvation. And it would be fitting if he did, for certainly it has been through the mis-use of aesthetics that he has floundered and foundered. Examine for instance how the invention of the guillotine was so widely and wildly received because it was clean swift and thorough in its lethal use. An aesthetic but with what as its product. Sudden death. The Nobel Peace Prize created by Alfred Nobel, a chemist, invented dynamite. It is used constructively and *destructively* by terrorists and assassins. I'm quite sure both uses are seen as *beautiful* when it carries out the intention behind it. And, isn't a huge brilliant mushroom of atomic gases and radiation seen as startlingly lovely to anyone who is many miles away. Do you think perhaps one consideration remains that many scientists loved the idea of "the bomb" and still do?

How can Man use aesthetics to send him toward a more desirable existence? For one, several hospitals have for some time arranged the playing of soothing music inside maternity wards, where the babies are discovered to be less colic, less temperamental. They rest longer and better. This has now evolved into the additional discovery that it works for most patients in hospital type atmospheres. What person doesn't feel more tranquil, even more alive in front of and viewing a fine painter's masterpiece. I get that way seeing that quality of art reproduced in a digital form as well. We're noticing an upswing in LIVE television programming where dancing and vocalizing is praised copiously and the artists get better and better as the

shows continue. We should never pass up the occasion to comple-
ment a quality product or service. That is the aesthetic we want to en-
courage.

Lastly there is *beauty* to self mastery. Poets and philosophers
have written and spoken of it a myriad number of times. It is possibly
a goal which if a larger proportion of our society made it there duty
to accomplish, concurrently we would see a swift rise in the culture's
stability.

POETRY MY MOTHER
WOULD'VE APPROVED

C. VAN HEYDEN

Pick up your copy of the companion book of poetry, and get
ready for the next in series:
POETRY YOUR MOTHER WOULD NOT HAVE APPROVED

Now Available at Amazon.com